SCARLET LINES

P.K.Jha

Clever Fox
PUBLISHING

Chennai • Bangalore

CLEVER FOX PUBLISHING
Chennai, India

Published by CLEVER FOX PUBLISHING 2022
Copyright © P.K.Jha 2022

All Rights Reserved.
ISBN: 978-93-94457-97-3

This book is dedicated to all those whose illnesses cannot be seen. To all those who struggle with addiction. To all those whose problems just lie in their heads. To all those who have seen the face of death and survived. And to those who did not.

This book showcases a few events that I have lived through. I have not exaggerated or dulled down anything. The only changes that have been made are because of storytelling purposes. Consider this your trigger warning for substance abuse, self-harm and suicide. I have made it as graphic as I witnessed it.

CONTENTS

1

GOD

*"H*ey, man. Do we have anymore?" asked A.

I was quite confused hearing this, as we had bought 5 grams the previous night. There is no way that we would have gone through all of it between just the three of us. As I walked to the table where we were snorting our lines, I was surprised to see that there was just a bit left which A was cutting into 3 lines. After snorting my line, I made a strong drink of rum and coke, and so did the others. We were not saying anything, but we were definitely thinking the same thing. No one wanted to be the first one to admit that we needed more cocaine.

B was the first to crack, after only 4 sips into his drink. He casually asked us if we wanted to end the night here or shall we continue. Both A and I just jumped to get our phones to see which dealers were working without even saying a word. Dealer 1 did not respond, but dealer 2 replied almost immediately. I was a bit apprehensive about dealer 2. Last time, he sold some very bad coke to me but A reassured me that dealer 2 got a new batch which was pretty good. As we had no other options, we ordered 3 grams, to which dealer 2 just replied with a thumb's up emoji. He knew my address already and would generally come within 30 minutes. And these 30 minutes are what I hated the most about doing drugs.

While waiting for our coke, all of us finished our drinks and I took the job of refilling them. I walked to the kitchen counter after collecting the cups from A and B, then, it just hits me. I had not slept for a week now. This thought was kind of concerning, but I did not bother to care.

I have gained somewhat of a reputation for making strong drinks. But at that moment, I was so high that strong just would not cut it. So, I made the drinks in the proportion of 60-40, 60 rum and 40 Coca-Cola. I gave the drinks to my friends, and from the look on their faces after drinking their first sip, I don't think they appreciated it.

I was a bit zoned out from the conversation A and B were having when B caught my attention and asked, "Hey P, you have not been able to sleep for a long time now. Are you sure you are good? Maybe you need to see a doctor or at least stop doing drugs?"

I had been hearing these questions from this man every 5 hours, and I really did not want to humour him anymore so I told him to stop annoying me. He looked offended by my reaction but I was not bothered by that. I just did not want him to continue the conversation. He dramatically took a sip of his drink like he had something inspiring to say. But thankfully dealer 2 saved me from the preaching by ringing the bell.

I opened the door and welcomed him in. This dealer had known us for the past couple of years and was very friendly with us, but most importantly, he was professional and did not like to waste time. He walked in, greeted all of us, took out a big bag of coke and handed it to me as I was trying to collect the cash to give him. He said that he put in a little extra, so we thanked him, gave him the cash, and he was on his way.

As soon as he left, I walked up to the mirror on which we were doing coke, poured all of it out of the bag, and started crushing it. The consistency with which it was being crushed was perfect. It also had the best aroma that I could have smelled at that time. After making it into a fine powder, I made three reasonably same-sized lines, took my straw and snorted the line on the left with my right nostril. It had a slight burn to it, but as soon as I got up, I could feel the dopamine rushing to the brain. I could taste the coke in my throat, and just like that, my life was beautiful again.

I reminded A and B who were in a random conversation at this point that their lines are waiting for them on the table. Now, I wanted nothing more than a cigarette to savour the moment.

I could not find my lighter so I lit my cigarette from the stove. As soon as that first puff hit, it felt like the sweet taste of death pairing beautifully with the taste of coke already present in my throat.

A and B took their lines, sat back on the couch and started drinking again.

"See, I told you this batch was good," said A.

I nodded in agreement while holding a drink in one hand and a cigarette in another.

B never really could stop talking when we were doing coke, and once again he started talking about a topic I was not really interested in, which was religion. I was not a religious man myself, but I had a phase of learning more about it, however, I was completely over that phase. But sometimes it could turn out to be a nice conversation, so I tried to hear what he had to say.

B preached, "Even though none of us believes in God, can we be sure that this is the right mindset to have?

Presuming that we get undeniable proof that God does not exist, should we not believe in God still? If believing in something which might or might not exist makes us more motivated, or in some sense even happier, is it not logical to believe in God?"

A weirdly had a reply ready for this. "What you are saying is true when we do not look at the caveats like organised religion is way more than just God. It takes more from you than it can give. On the other side, we have spirituality which feels like something appropriate for this line of thought, but in the end, it has become an organised religion of its own."

The conversation was getting too intense. I sneakily went to make some more lines while they argued.

B added, "I am not trying to say that we look at God in the same manner as religion, but rather look at it as something earthly, which could be physical or metaphysical. For example, some people could find God in money, beauty, art, and so on. Maybe God is something which makes you feel satisfied with your life."

That last sentence that B said really stuck with me. I did my line and a single thought came into my mind. I have been happy all of my life, my friends and family have been perfect but still, I don't think I have ever felt satisfied. Whenever I had less, I wanted more. Whenever

I had more, I wanted less. This applied to everything I have experienced in my life. May it be love, happiness, or sleep. Thus, in that drunk, high and sleep-deprived state I decided that I am going to get satisfied, and I am going to find my God.

I wanted to stay alone with this thought in my head as it was extremely exciting, but for that, I had to kick my friends out which was easier than it seemed. I just had to say that I felt like I need to sleep, and their fake concern was kind enough to let me be.

As soon as they left, I got the coke to the couch, put on some shitty reality TV show, and spent my night doing coke and thinking about God to the background noises of the TV.

2

MANIA

I tried to snort some more coke, but I was physically unable to. My nostrils were swollen up from the days of drug abuse to a point that they could not snort anything anymore. I thought blowing my nose would create a small passageway, from my nose to my brain. I took some tissues from the kitchen and blew my nose on them with all my might. My nose excreted all the snot it had, the only problem being, it was red in colour. It was not a good sign that my nostrils had started bleeding, because the blood would clot, making it harder to snort. I blew out one nostril at a time to figure out where the problem lied. My left nostril only had some snot mixed with coke to offer, while the right one was spraying out blood. This information was really helpful in deciding which nostril to use to do the coke.

I brought the mirror on which we were doing coke to the coffee table, which was in front of the couch. I made two lines hoping that my nose had the power to inhale them. For the first one, I snorted easily through my left nostril. The second one took three tries to snort, but I did manage to do it.

Even though I could snort the coke, it had stopped giving me any sort of high. Probably because my dopamine receptors were overworked. I had started to crash, and I was crashing hard. It was impossible for me to fall asleep, so I did not even try. I thought of taking my anti-anxiety pills to calm down the situation. It may even help me sleep. However, I was liking the feeling of nothingness in my head. My mind wandered into a little dark room, which it did not want to leave. The only problem was that I was low on energy. And my usual energy fuelling powder had stopped working.

I needed to be creative to find a solution, so I poured myself a drink to get my creative juices flowing. There were not a lot of options in my head, and only one of those was possible. It was the one thing I dreaded the most in the world, but it was the only thing that would keep me going. I needed to take a shower.

I slowly finished my drink and lit up a cigarette, still contemplating the decision that I had made. There was no running away from that excruciating experience anymore. I put out my cigarette and went to the shower with my phone.

I put on my playlist on the phone, stepped under the running water like a zombie, and did not move. To be honest, I was so physically drained that I don't know if I could have moved even if I wanted to. The only thing that kept me even standing was the music being played, and as soon as that thought entered my head, like God controlling the playlist, it played the one song that I needed at that moment. Boris Nuts by Monkey 3.

With every note of that song, I could feel energy rushing through my body. My hands started shaking, and my mind was experiencing pure euphoria. I knew this feeling very well; I was starting to get manic. In that moment of bliss, I thanked my brain for my mental illness.

My manic episodes had always ended very badly. I had to make a decision; whether I was going to stop it right where it was, or let it take control of my body. The song still being played in the background was biasing a very important decision. The notes of the song hitting me through the waterfall of the shower, made me feel a better high than any drug I had ever done. I was rational enough to know the end result of playing with my illness, but the addict in me needed more of the sweet elixir my brain could make for free. In the fight between my rational and addict self, the addict came on top, as always.

I got out of the shower and without even getting dressed, tried to figure out how to keep this mania going, because I knew I could get higher than this, and also that I could crash any minute. I knew some of the triggers which kept me manic, but it was just the right combination of these triggers that I needed.

The triggers that I knew of ranged from hearing certain songs, and watching specific films, to harming myself physically or mentally. But the best mania that I had ever felt was in between the time of deciding to commit suicide and trying to commit suicide.

I tried to be smart about the situation and introduced my triggers slowly. I put on the basement sessions by Radiohead on the speaker, and just lay on the bed to let Thom Yorke's voice do its magic. I tried to slowly get lost in my thoughts when suddenly I remembered that I was on a quest for God, and being manic was definitely the state in which I wanted to take this journey.

I wanted to make a mental list of what I would be able to consider God. The first candidate was art. It may be music, movies or just paintings. Any and all form of art had the ability to transport me to a different space, which I considered to be very God-like. The only problem with art was that it was created by humans, and if art was God, then the creator of the art is also God. I was not at all happy with the idea of humans being God, but it was an interesting idea for later.

The second candidate that I thought of was love. I had experienced love for only a few people in my life, and maybe for cocaine, but the whole concept of loving people had the exact same problems as loving cocaine. Even though I claimed I loved coke, the truth was that I was addicted to it. Which bought up the question of the difference between love and addiction. To claim that I love my family the most would also mean that I am only addicted to them because I have known them for my entire life. And if someone I loved were to leave my life, I could associate my sadness with withdrawals from that addiction.

Now, could addiction in itself be a candidate? I had a hard time believing so because I could get myself addicted to anything that I wanted to, making the object of addiction my God. It would also mean that in the case of addiction to people or love, humans would be God. Coming back to the same problem I faced with art, it did not seem to be the answer. This thought was not even worth coming back to.

While looking for the next candidate for God, Radiohead stopped playing from the speakers, and my phone started to vibrate. It was the call of C. I liked

C. I had not seen C in a long time and was pleasantly surprised by the call.

I answered the phone and greeted him. He told me he had been away for a while and just got back last night. He then proceeded to tell me that he has got forty tabs of LSD with him and asked me if I wanted to do some. I immediately said yes, to which he asked me to come over to his house. I said that I would be there in about an hour and hung up.

I had not done any psychedelics for a couple of years. I was one of those people who were not supposed to do psychedelics; my psychiatrist had told me that very firmly. But I had only stopped because after my last trip of magic mushroom, I had to be involuntarily admitted to a psychiatric hospital for a month.

I knew I was making a bad decision but it seemed like something which would trigger my mania even more. Maybe I could even find God on it as many people do.

So, I got up from my bed, took a shot of vodka, did a line of coke and was on my way for a magical experience.

3

PSYCHEDELICS

*O*n entering Cs's apartment, I was quite surprised. He was not someone who would put a lot of effort into anything, but the living room looked like psychedelic heaven. There were different coloured lights, glowsticks arranged in random shapes and most importantly a lot of blankets and pillows arranged in a manner to kind of look like a pillow fort.

As I was about to ask the reason behind this elaborate setup, D came out of the bedroom. D was C's girlfriend who would always try to make drug experiences as nice as possible; probably because she was new to doing drugs.

"So, what do you think about our psychedelic palace?" asked D giggling.

It was definitely better than the crack house vibe I was expecting, but I ignored her question and went on to ask C how strong these tabs were. He said that the dealer claimed it to be around 220 micrograms, however, he had tried them a couple of weeks ago, and thought that they were close to 180. Both those numbers seemed fine to me. I asked D, "Are you doing a full tab?" She sighed, "Sadly I am not doing any. I have a meeting tomorrow, so I will just tripsit you.".

A knock on the door interrupted the conversation. It was A. I was not expecting anyone else to join us but it did not make any difference. A got into the living room and saw the 'psychedelic palace'. He thanked D for setting it up and tripsitting us. D was happy that someone was grateful for her work.

C exclaimed, "Are we ready to see a new world?" and without saying a word all of us sat in the pillow fort. C got his drug box out, which had maybe 10 different research chemicals in it, and also a sheet of acid. We took 3 tabs out of the sheet.

"See you on the other side," A said while letting out a big sigh, and we put the tabs on our tongues.

I took the responsibility of playing music for the night and started playing some Pink Floyd. A, C and D gave me some suggestions to put on the queue which I hesitantly did.

30 minutes after taking the tabs A inquired, "Were you able to sleep last night?". I lied and said yes to avoid any further questioning of my state of mind.

Hearing that question D asked me, "Are you in a decent state of mind to be doing psychedelics?"

"Isn't it a bit too late to ask that question?" I smirked and replied.

D jokingly said that I was stupid, and put her hands on the table. I saw her neon green nail paint leave traces in the whole journey of her hand. I knew that I had started tripping.

Before I could say anything, A said, "Did anyone else see that?"

"You mean the nails, right?" C replied.

All three of us looked at each other and started laughing. C let us know that the song being played was his suggestion. He had heard this song at a rave and swore that it shot his trip up. I was a bit apprehensive, but with every beat of the song, I could feel the room pulsating more and more. By the end of the six minutes, the cows in C's painting were dancing.

This seemed like the perfect time to smoke a cigarette. I somehow got up and tried to walk to the balcony. On opening the doors to the balcony, a cool breeze embraced me, giving me goosebumps. I was able to light my cigarette on the 3rd try, and the taste seemed heavenly. It seemed like I could taste every colour I was seeing in the smoke of my cigarette. When I looked up at the stars, the taste of the cigarette also became glittery, moving around my mouth. The light on the cigarette was making patterns I had never seen in my life. It was such a beautiful thing that I did not want it to end, but I respected it enough to not light another one.

On re-joining the group, I saw that they were playing with some toys like they were kids. I was not interested in toys at that moment so I laid down on the couch and tried to find the prettiest hallucination I was having. It was very close between the dancing cows and the traces of my hand, but the traces had won.

The game in my head was interrupted by D. "I have a gift for all of you," she said.

All of us got very excited on hearing that. She pulled a bag of ecstasy and asked us if we wanted to candyflip. It had been about three hours into the trip, and none of us had our brains working at full capacity. We did not even need to discuss it to agree to it.

D passed the bag around the circle for the three of us to take a pill, starting from C, then A, and I finally got the bag. I saw it had 2CB in it too. So, I sneakily took one of each pill and downed it with water. Surprisingly no one noticed, and I went back to looking at hand traces.

A few minutes after popping those pills I started to get a bit anxious, thinking if I had made a bad decision. I knew that it was the come-up anxiety of ecstasy, but I was not in the state of mind to rationalize through it. I did the only thing which made sense at that moment, to play the song Echoes by Pink Floyd. Its familiarity calmed me down while making fractals in my vision. As the song progressed to the 10-minute mark, I knew I was being transported to a different realm; the fractals got more vivid, colours that I had never seen before started to appear, and as the song reached its finale after 23 minutes, it seemed like I was inside a very fast spinning disco ball.

My mind had left the room that I was in, it was wandering to the new frontiers of time and space. I did not have any sense of myself at that moment, so much so that I could not move my body as I wanted to. I tried to move my legs and stand up to go smoke, but even though I could feel my legs move, I saw that they were stationary. I wanted to ask my friends if they feel anything new, but I could not open my mouth to talk. The only moment that my body allowed was for my hand to see the pretty traces.

In my somewhat state of paralysis, a fly flew through my vision. At that moment it seemed like a message from God, and that I still needed to find it. God had allowed me to move once again, and with my newfound appreciation for movement, I went to smoke another cigarette.

This cigarette seemed very different from the last one. It seemed to provide me with life itself, and at that moment, it was my God. I could still taste the colours and the stars in the cigarette, but this one was holy in all senses. It gave my life purpose while I gave its life purpose, at the same time trying to kill each other. It gave me something and it took something from me, and the balance between the two made it so beautiful. I tried to write that thought on my phone for a time when I am sober as I knew this is how I will find the main God of my life. But it was impossible for me to write on my phone so I tried very hard to make a mental note of it and joined the group once again.

D asked me if I was all right, she was concerned because I had not said anything in a while. I reassured her that I was having a fun time playing with my mind, and looked over to see A and C watching 'trippy' videos on a phone. I asked D if there was something fun to eat in the house, I wanted to experience eating in this state.

"Sure!" she said and ran to the kitchen. She came back and much to my surprise, put a lot of magic mushrooms on the coffee table in front of me. I glared at her.

She smiled at me and muttered, "Could be fun." A and C saw those and made clear that they would not be partaking in the mushrooms, so I had a decision to make. Even in my fucked-up state I knew it was a bad decision, and I will probably regret it. So, I tackled that dilemma like I tackle every drug dilemma, by doing more drugs.

I ate about one-third of the pile on the table, and the texture of the mushrooms was just the perfect thing to chew on. It felt like a whole ecosystem was thriving in my mouth while eating them, which led me to go for more and more. And just like that all of them were gone.

I took back my position on the couch looking at traces of my hand. I had lost all comprehension of time, but it had manifested in another way in my body. I could feel the mushrooms inside me growing, and with every unit of growth, my metaphysical self was leaving my physical self, till the point, the mushroom grew to its full state, and I knew nothing about my body.

I tried to think about what was happening to me but my inner monologue could not grasp the concept of language. My vision was filled with just lights of different colours blinking in a room I had never been in. I could hear different sounds but it was impossible for me to make sense of it. And my mind was nowhere to be found.

After spending some unknown amount of time in this state, I heard a voice that made sense. It was not the voice of anyone in the physical room with me, still, I recognised it. It was X who was talking to me. I had not heard X in a couple of years since I had started to take my medication regularly. But here he was, striking when I was at my most vulnerable.

X greeted me like a friend, he had a habit of doing that. He asked me how my search for God was going. Ignoring the question, I told him that I sometimes missed him, to which he very convincingly stated to stop taking my medication.

He added, "I can help you find your God, even though I have already told you many times what you are looking for."

I knew what he was talking about, the only purpose of his in my life was to convince me to die. Hence making death my God. I told him that I did not believe it to be possible, even though I could feel in my bones that this could be true.

He said, "If you ever need me, you know what to do."

He was hinting that I should stop my medication. I waited for him to continue the conversation but he had gone.

Suddenly I was transported back to the physical world and felt quite sober. A and C seemed sober too while D was making some tea. I asked them, "what happened? How are we sober so fast?"

A replied, "Bro, you dozed off on the couch for a couple of hours so we let you be. It has been almost 12 hours since we did the tab of acid."

I did not know if I had slept or just had spent all my time with X, but whatever it might be my body seemed to appreciate any amount of sleep after so long. D asked, "Do you want some tea too?", which I declined saying, "I would rather go home and rest some more." I said my goodbyes and was on my way home.

On the walk to my apartment, I could still see some mild hallucinations which made my city way prettier than it was. I tried to make sense of whatever happened the previous night but my brain felt completely overworked and scrambled.

Upon reaching my apartment, I took out a sandwich from the fridge and had a couple of bites. But my stomach started to repulse anything going into it. My stomach started to growl, and it felt like I was going to throw up, so I ran to the bathroom. But nothing was coming out of me, just dry heaves. I went back to my room and saw my medications lying on my bedside table. I approached them thinking, this is something I cannot fuck around with. I took all 8 pills in one hand, went to the kitchen, and filled a glass with water. I looked at all those colourful pills for maybe a minute. I knew this moment would define my life going forward. I chose to take the road with more risks and chucked all those pills in the bin.

4

PLEASURE

The psychedelic debacle drained my life from me. Not only was I less manic, but I felt no sensation of pleasure or even pain. I tried to sleep without any great success, even put on some Netflix to let this comedown pass, but it was not of any help either. I needed some sort of stimulation to kickstart my mania again, and so I turned to the leftover coke I had on my table.

I made three small lines and snorted them one after the other. My body started tingling, but not in a good way. The adverse effects of the lack of food in my stomach were much more than what I wanted to deal with. My body was rejecting the cocaine in the form of nausea, so I needed to find a solution that would work for both me and my body. It occurred to me that if I lowered my body's inhibitions, it would have a hard time rejecting anything that I put into it. Hence, I made a strong drink and took a big gulp of it. Nausea only increased because of this action, to a point that I could taste vomit in my mouth.

I started looking for my cigarettes as they were the only physical object which could keep the puke down. Upon finding them, I lit one, and slowly savoured the little dance with death. The cigarette did its job of suppressing the need to throw up, so I took another sip of the drink to check if nausea would return. It did not. I finished my drink, and put my focus on cocaine. I made a small line, which made me high, but not as much as I wanted it to.

I proceeded to gather my thoughts about the trip I had been on while lighting up a cigarette. The taste of the cigarette had the residue of the glittery colours I had felt in my mouth. I remembered a certain point when I thought that a cigarette might be my God. It seemed like a preposterous idea to my sober self at first, but as I thought more about it, not just cigarettes, but most of my vices including alcohol and drugs could be seen as my God in a certain sense. This theory made even more sense because I had credited drugs for the reason of keeping me alive multiple times, however ironic that may be.

I had always seen these vices as only a form of pleasure which made me deflect from considering them as my God. But only now did I realize that my God would be the highest form of pleasure in itself. This begged the question of rating the different forms of pleasure I indulged in. I was happy to have progressed so far and decided to reward myself with another line.

Even though I was drinking alcohol for the easy consumption of coke, the coke in itself was not giving me the same high as it normally would, it was better than nothing though.

The only question lingering in my head was, how much of pleasure is coke for me? There was no simple answer for that, which led me to go back to the time when coke kind of saved my life.

A couple of years ago, I was completely off my meds for a very long time and might have been in a state of psychosis. Nothing made sense to me, and the question of life or death was very heavily discussed in my mind. Not because I did not want to live or I was in a great deal of pain, but simply because I was completely bored of life. Nothing in my life gave me any pleasure except alcohol, cocaine and cigarettes. These were the three heroes who pulled me back from death.

Fun times, I thought. I made another drink in honour of cocaine. It was obvious to me that the story of coke saving my life had my answer hidden in it. On a closer inspection of that time, some things started to get clear.

I had used coke to get me out of the mundaneness of life. I was probably still using coke for the same reason. Looking at it from a different perspective, I used it as a form of entertainment. I always gave it more meaning in my life, but in the end, it was just a different form of Netflix. Alcohol was mostly the same. Also, both of these pleasures gave me artificial highs, when I knew my God would give me the most perfect and natural high.

Cigarettes, on the other hand, felt different. They were not just a form of entertainment, but rather a reason to stay alive by themselves. Smoking did not make me high, though it provided me with a lot of pleasure. Definitely, more pleasure than any sort of entertainment could have provided me. So, it was only logical to keep cigarettes above entertainment on my pleasure list.

This train of thought made my lungs itch to be burned. They needed to play dice with death itself as they had been corrupted, and just oxygen did not let them be satisfied. I looked at my pack of Marlboro Reds, took out a single cigarette, and cherished my relationship with it. I had often thought, it was the only thing in my life that would never betray me and is not in the disguise of a friend, like drugs and alcohol. I put it in my mouth and lit the other end. We were in perfect harmony. My relationship with it seemed almost sexual, maybe I was even deriving sexual pleasure from it, which I could not from people. It made me think of how people say pure sexual pleasure is only derived from love. Maybe a cigarette was the only thing I had ever loved.

While engaged with my love, my eyes went over to some old friends. The pile of coke and the bottle of alcohol almost lost all value to me. A veil had been lifted from my eyes and they seemed so dirty. They were like houseguests who simply never left. Even though I knew now that my love for them was just an illusion, I was still not going to kick them out, as I still could not bear that loss. I decided to keep on indulging in them. They might just be entertainment, but I needed to be entertained.

I celebrated the recent round of revelations with another drink and three more lines. However, the magic of such substances had disappeared at that moment. The only thing I could feel was the comedown of coke, with the high nowhere in sight. It was not the first time it had happened, but unlike the other times, this comedown was taking my mania with it, and just in a couple of minutes, not only was I not high on coke, but I was also not manic at all. I could not feel, and hence I could not think.

This had to change, it was the only way of life I knew now. I had stopped my medication. So, I knew it would be easy to get back to the state, therefore I started playing with my triggers. I played Exit music by Radiohead, lit up another cigarette, and just waited for the beauty of the song to cast its spell. The song was over at the same moment as my cigarette; however, I had no rush of dopamine in my brain. I tried again with the strongest song in my repertoire, Mind Flowers by Ultimate Spinach, but the result was no different. I started to panic a bit, my body started feeling the effects of not sleeping and being on a drug binge for a long time. I had to do something fast. My go-to option here generally was to watch a great film and kickstart my mania using the high that I always got after watching a pure piece of art. Unfortunately, I did not have time for that. I knew what I had to do, something I had not done in years, but it was the only thing that would help. I had to hurt myself.

I went to the kitchen and saw that all my knives were dirty from the meal I had made 3 weeks ago. I took the sharpest knife I had and went to the sink to clean it. Within seconds the craving to be high got so powerful that I did not even clean it properly. Right there in the kitchen I pulled up my sleeve, and cut lightly on my arm, just below my shoulder. This action pumped dopamine into my brain. It could have been enough to get my mania going, but I had forgotten how good cutting felt. I waited a few seconds and cut once again below the first one, a bit deeper this time. I could feel my brain releasing all the happy chemicals. I had found a long-lost love again. I made the third cut, going very deep. What I felt was nothing short of ecstasy, not the drug, but divine ecstasy. I reluctantly stopped at 3. I played Exit Music once again and lit up a cigarette once again. But this time when they ended together, I was the king of the world.

5

PARTY

*M*aybe X was right in suggesting that I stop taking my medication. No drug or any combination of them could make me feel this way. It was enough to consider if this was it. Was mania my ultimate God? Was this my reason for being? I found this concept to be very hard to fathom. I had only tasted bits of mania called 'hypomania' by the doctors, only now after years had I experienced the full thing. I needed some time with it to know if this is what I was looking for.

Gathering myself together I saw that my physical body was also reacting to the full-blown manic episode I was feeling. My hands were shaking, my stomach was wrenching and my whole vision had a tint of orange like I had worn orange-tinted glasses. I took a few steps and lit another cigarette to calm my body down. But it was just restless, I needed to do something, something which would keep on fuelling the fire in my brain. After a long time, I *wanted* to see other people and just do something stupid.

I picked up my phone and started going through my contacts. When I saw B's number on my phone, I knew he was the perfect person to contact. Even though I did not like him very much, he was always down for anything. I called him, but he did not answer. So, I left him a message asking what he was doing. I resumed drinking alcohol, waiting for his reply. A couple of minutes later I got a call back from B. He was in a place with loud music.

I asked him, "What are you up to?", to which he screamed over the music, "There is a party at my house, you should come over."

His words were like words of God itself. A party sounded great to me. The perfect place for my manic self. I told him that I would be there as soon as I can and hung up. The thought of a party had blood rushing to my head, and I straight away started getting ready to go over there. I asked myself whether I should shower, but the idea did not excite me. I finished the drink that I had made, did a couple more lines of coke to get the mood going, put on some shoes and I was ready.

On the walk to B's place, the thought of God entered my head once again. If God is the highest form of pleasure, it could not be mania in itself. Mania, as good as it made me feel, gave me a sense of extreme restlessness, which would defeat the purpose of the highest pleasure. But if I take the restlessness away, then it definitely would be what I was looking for. The way for that was quite obvious, and also the beauty of mania, that I could mix any number of pleasures with it. It would only make sense for my God to be mania mixed with another form or forms of lower pleasures.

Halfway to B's apartment, my thought went on to the party, and if I could find some meaningful insights over there. The idea of interacting with people was very amusing. I had a general disdain for people, but my manic self took great pleasure from them. It could be possible that society, from which I rarely took pleasure, merged with mania is what I was looking for. It was a nice thought to ponder upon, and I was going to put it to the test.

Outside B's apartment, a group of people were smoking. On approaching them, one of them asked me if I was there for the party. I lit up a cigarette and told him that I was. He was delighted by that answer and handed me the bottle of wine he was drinking from. I took a swig from it and handed it back.

I asked him, "How is it up there?"

With a look of approval, he said, "It's buzzing."

His friends called him back at this point to discuss someone's break-up. I put out my cigarette without finishing it and entered B's apartment.

As I walked through the hallway, I could hear music coming from the last door on the right. If someone did not know where exactly B lived, they were not going to have any problem finding it. His door was ajar. I went into a room with very heavy EDM music being played on huge speakers. In between the speakers, there was a man with a DJ set. The only lights on the sea of people dancing were the moving lasers. There must have been 70 people there. I walked into the dancers to make my way to the kitchen on the opposite side of the dance floor. I somehow managed to make it.

I knew almost no one at this party, but somehow, I managed to find A in the kitchen. He poured me a drink and tried to say something to me, but the blasting music made it impossible for me to understand him. I actioned that I could not hear him, to which he gestured me to follow him with his hands. I picked up my drink and followed him to B's bedroom.

In the room, there were four people around a chair on which B was sitting, facing the table. He turned around to see me and expressed that he was glad that I could come. Behind him, on the table, there was a Calculus book with about a gram of coke on it.

I laughingly asked, "It's that time already then?"

He smirkingly replied, "That time never stopped."

He introduced me to the other people in the room. He knew them from his courses at the university, and this was the birthday party of one of the girls in the room. I greeted her with happy birthday and expressed my gratitude for having me. She said, "Thank you. As the clock just hit 12 a couple of minutes ago, would you mind making me my birthday line? And make one for you too."

I chuckled and muttered, "Your wish is my command." I continued to make two lines on the book, and handed her the straw saying, "Birthday girl goes first."

She took the straw, put her hair in a bun so it doesn't wipe the rest of the coke away, and smoothly snorted it. She handed me back the straw while smiling at me. I bent down and railed my fat line. The coke felt way better than what I was doing at home. I immediately felt it numbing my throat and adding high to my mania.

B asked me if I could make lines for everyone in the room. I counted the number of people to be 7 and went to work. I made five lines and saw that I needed to crush a bit more to make 7. But as I was feeling lazy, I decided to cheat and made two more lines taking a bit from the other five. The general rule was that the person who makes the line takes the first one, except for special occasions, but the birthday girl had her go already, so I picked the one which looked the fattest and snorted that. I moved from the table to give everyone their chance to do their lines. The birthday girl went second and joined me in the back of the room.

She asked me," How do you know B?". I thought about that question for a second, but I did not really know the answer to it.

I told her, "I don't really know, I think he just randomly started coming over to my place, but I don't know who invited him there the first time."

"So, do you always just become friends with random people who come over to your place?" she asked, laughing.

"Yeah. That is how I make most of my friends," I replied.

Interrupting the conversation, B, who was very visibly high at this point asked if we wanted another line. Both of us said yes at the same time.

While B was crushing the coke, I inquired the birthday girl, "So, apart from coke what other drugs or pleasures do you indulge in?"

She pondered for a second before saying, "I do like psychedelics quite a lot, but other than that coke it is for me. And about other pleasures, I gain deep pleasure from movies and there is nothing up there with smoking a cigarette."

I was quite happy with that answer, so I asked her if she wanted to join me for a smoke on the balcony after doing our lines. She happily agreed.

B was taking a long time to make the lines, probably because he was busy talking to the other people in the room. I asked him if he was done, to which he snorted a line and passed me the straw. I did mine, and suddenly I was very high. I waited for the birthday girl to do hers and went out of the room to go to the balcony. There were fewer people on the dance floor which made it easier to go through, but the music was still so loud that it gave me a headache.

On the balcony, I took out two cigarettes, gave one to the birthday girl, lit her cigarette with my lighter, and proceeded to light mine. She enquired about my life a bit, to which I had no problem sharing the details to, but she ended up with a simple question, "What do you do?"

"What I did was far more important that any job or degree. I was on a quest for God." I would have never said these thoughts to another person, but I was so high that the words just came out of my mouth.

She seemed very interested in that answer and asked me to explain further.

I told her that I thought every person has their form of God. For me, it would be my highest form of pleasure, and that is what I was looking for. She asked if I had found something of that sort.

I told her, "I have been given a curse and boon in the form of my mental illness. Let's forget the curse part for now, but the boon is called mania. It makes me higher than any drug in this world. I think that is the answer. But in itself, it feels incomplete, so I am looking for something to go with it."

"I think this is such an interesting thought. I have a friend who has bipolar disorder, and I have heard similar things about her mania. Are you in a manic episode now?" she inquired.

I chuckled, "Yeah, definitely."

She expressed her fascination with my line of thought. She wanted to know what I was thinking of mixing with mania.

I told her, "It has to be a type of pleasure. I have categorized and put entertainment at the bottom of my list, which also includes drugs and alcohol. A cigarette is at the top at this moment, and now I am testing how the pleasure of society turns out to be."

She took a drag of her cigarette, and pointed out, "If you are categorizing drugs and alcohol as entertainment, should society or let's say people in general not be categorised the same? Obviously, society is needed to function to the fullest, but I don't think you are counting necessities as pleasure, otherwise, food and water would also come into play. Additionally, taking the necessity part apart, is society anything else but entertainment?"

I was extremely impressed by this line of thought. I expressed, "Wow! You are absolutely right. I don't know why I did not think of that. But if people are just entertainment, then there is no point of me being here."

She annoyingly grinned, "I did not take you to be that stupid. Even if people are entertainment, what is wrong with being entertained? You are still drinking and doing drugs, right? So, why do you want to leave people? Now finish your cigarette and come dance with me."

She made absolute sense. I flicked my cigarette out the balcony to go to the dance floor with the birthday girl.

The music had calmed down, and the dance floor was almost empty.

She said, "I don't think this is going to be fun anymore, might as well just do a line, right?"

I willingly agreed and walked toward B's room.

B shouted, "Right on time for the last lines."

He went on to add two lines on the book, and all of us took turns to do the deed. After that, I asked the birthday girl, "Would you be interested in coming back to my place to keep the conversation going? I would love to talk to you some more."

She answered, "I was waiting for that question. Yeah, it would be really nice. I also have more coke to keep us going."

6

BIRTHDAY GIRL

On the way back to my apartment, the birthday girl and I stopped every few minutes to do a bump of coke from my key. We did not talk much during most of the walk. But when I asked why she was with a random person she met at a party on her birthday, she shrugged and let me know that she was new in the city.

She confessed, "I have made some friends here, but only because I don't want to be alone. I have not found anyone that I am actually fond of. The people I have found are very......I don't know the word, but just something which I don't desire at the moment. On the other hand, your crazy ideas seemed very interesting. I am sure talking about it would be more fun than going to a club or something."

I chuckled, "I am sure doing absolutely nothing would be better than going to the clubs."

Both of us laughed and did another bump right outside my door.

I was not expecting a guest when I left my house, which looked nothing less than a crack den. There were months-old bags of McDonald's that we had to cross to get to the living room. It smelled awful because I had not taken the trash out in weeks. There were about 15 bottles of alcohol at different places and on the coffee table was a mirror with a pile of coke on it. I apologised profusely about the condition of my apartment. I even told her that if I knew someone was coming here, I would have cleaned up, knowing very well that I definitely would not have. Surprisingly, she looked amused by what she was seeing, only to let me know that her house probably was in a worse state than this. I did not believe that for a second, but at least she was trying to be polite.

We took our seats on the couch, I connected my phone to the speaker and asked the birthday girl, "What kind of music do you like?".

She hesitantly answered, "I listen to a lot of psychedelic rock or something like Led Zeppelin, and even some new stuff like Mogwai, when I am by myself. But when I am around people, it doesn't matter. I don't really mind anything, so you can play whatever you want."

That answer resonated with me. We had almost the same taste in music, so in a slight attempt to impress her, I put on the album The Hawk Is Howling by Mogwai. She gave her approval with a smile.

"So, shall we?" she asked, pointing towards the mirror on the table.

"Yeah, sure. But your coke is way better than what I have here. Do you want to finish this and get on to that, or just get on with yours?" I inquired.

She put up a good point that the coke I had was already crushed, so we might as well just finish it. I obliged and made two lines on the mirror. I gestured to let her go first.

"The one who makes the line takes the first one," she insisted.

We did a couple of lines and made some small talk before she ended up asking me what kind of films I watch. I considered myself somewhat of a film fanatic, and hence that question lighted me up.

I responded, thinking vividly, "I think right now my favourite directors are Gaspar Noe and Lars Von Trier. I am also a huge fan of Ingmar Bergman, his work seems to take a part of my soul, which makes it a bit difficult to watch him. There is this one director Julia Ducournau, who made this film called *Raw*, which I think is my favourite film of the moment."

She was startled by the answer. She continued on this path by adding, "I have seen *Raw*, it is definitely spectacular. Have you seen this other film by Julia called *Titane*?"

I was embarrassed to say, "I watched almost half of it about a month ago, but I have not been in a state to complete it since."

She made a joking gesture of disappointment and asked me if I wanted another line. I simply nodded.

While she was cutting the lines, the album got over. The first album on my phone was Ok Computer by Radiohead, which I played without thinking much. The birthday girl looked at me while making the lines to give me a very agreeable nod. That put a smile on my face. We did our lines to continue our conversation.

"So, it obviously seems like you like films a lot, have you considered them to be your God maybe?" she asked.

I explained, "Films would be considered as a form of art. I thought about art being my form of God, but it did not make sense because in that case, the creator of the art would be God too. And that just doesn't sit well with me."

She took her time to consume that thought, and when she was ready, she surprised me by saying, "you said you are looking for pleasure to add with your mania. If you take the creator out of the picture and look at art as just a concept, it will provide a very good picture of pleasure. If we just stay on the topic of films as art, I also think the way it is consumed could make a difference in pleasure. For example, the logistics of direction and editing would provide a different kind of pleasure than the plot itself. I think what I am trying to say here is that there is a story, and there is a way the story is told. The symbiotic relationship between the two is where you should find your pleasure, leaving the creator behind. Moreover, art is a gateway to more pleasures. Staying on the topic of films, you can somewhat find out about different forms of pleasure without doing much work." She embarrassingly added, "Sorry if I am intruding too much. I am very high."

I reassured her telling, "No, you are definitely right. It is great to have someone to talk to about this and find good arguments. Which you certainly have in this case. I think I had tunnel vision going through this. I am going to take a look at art a bit further. Also, the thought of using films to explore different pleasures is genius. I am definitely going to do it. Thank you. Another line to celebrate?"

She chuckled, "I thought you would never ask."

The coke on the mirror was over so I asked her to get her bag out. She looked for it in her bag and handed it to me. I emptied the bag onto the mirror. There was just enough for two more lines each.

I started crushing it with my bank card when she suddenly asked, "You have probably gone through the basic pleasures like money or sex, right?"

I still intently crushing, answered, "If what I am looking for would be as basic as that, which I have dealt with my whole life, then I would already know it, right? I don't think it is worth wasting my time upon."

I finished crushing the coke and proceeded to make four big lines. "That's all we have for tonight," I said.

She positively replied, "It's fine, it was a good night."

I did my line and handed over the straw. She did hers and glared at the mirror only to say, "Wanna just go for the last one?"

I complied and did the last one of the night and so did she.

I informed the birthday girl that I had a tradition of drinking after finishing my coke. She happily obliged and asked if she could get a vodka and coke. I looked around for vodka in the room to find a bottle that had only enough to make two drinks. Maybe all this talk about God made it favour us. I made the drinks, got back to the couch and handed the birthday girl her drink, wishing her happy birthday once again. She seemed eager to continue our conversation, she asked what I felt about love.

I had the perfect answer to this. "Isn't love the same as addiction? Or as you said earlier that people are just entertainment. If that is true, then even the concept of love renders meaningless."

She did not seem satisfied with the answer. "Yeah, it does make sense that love is basically addiction, but I don't think that makes it meaningless. I am not even particularly talking about loving a person. You told me that you have put cigarettes high on the list of pleasures, and you do love or are addicted to them, whatever term you want to use. One could argue that the same goes for every pleasure there is, and the more you love something, the higher it is on your list of pleasures. I don't think it is a pleasure in itself, but the thing you are looking for might be the thing you love the most. It could lead you to what you want."

I was genuinely so impressed by her, which I had not felt for any human in a very long time. I let her know of this, and she as always just smiled at me.

She asked if she could steal a cigarette while our drinks were almost over. I gave her one with a lighter, and we both smoked in complete silence. We finished our drinks and our cigarettes, and the comedown of the coke was apparent. She asked if she could sleep over.

I said, "Why not?"

She went to bed, while I stayed on the couch. She yelled why was I not coming? I let her know that I have not been able to sleep in a long time, and I will just be up and bored in bed. She requested to just cuddle with her until she sleeps, which I had no problem with. We talked some more while she was slowly dozing off, and as she was completely asleep, I felt my body being pulled in by the bed. And to my surprise, I fell asleep.

7

BEAUTY

I suddenly felt a jerk in my sleep which woke me up. I opened my eyes to see the birthday girl sleeping next to me. The lights were turned off in my room, which was weird because they were on when I went to sleep. I disregarded it thinking that the birthday girl might have woken up sometime in between and turned them off. I started to feel a bit thirsty so I tried to get my bottle from the side table, but like a living nightmare, I could not move. My body felt completely paralyzed no matter how hard I tried to move. It made me think if I was dreaming. But I was in the exact same room that I was so familiar with; it was too vivid to not be the reality. I closed my eyes hoping it would just be a dream, but upon closing my eyes flashes of bright light seemed to pass through my room. I opened my eyes once again to investigate, only to see a shadowy figure with the face of a scary bunny sitting on my chest, slowly clapping. I freaked out. I wanted to scream and run, but no matter what I did, I could not move or make a sound to wake up the birthday girl. The only defence I had was to close my eyes, which I did, but something in my bones was asking me to open my eyes once again. I gathered some courage and opened my eyes to see that the bunny man was not sitting on me, but rather hovering right above me. Its nose almost touched my nose, and its toes almost touched my toes. Seeing that my ability to close my eyes was also taken away from me, I just looked at it, lying there helpless while trying to scream. Suddenly, the lights were turned on in the room, which gave me the power to scream, which I did like my life depended on it. My body just jolted out of the bed, and everything was back to normal. The birthday girl woke up with a concern, asking what happened to me. I told her I experienced a bad case of sleep paralysis. She worriedly asked me if I was fine.

I assured her, "Yeah, now I am good. It was just pretty intense for a second."

"Well, we are up now, and it is kind of morning already. Do you want to just stay up, and maybe eat some breakfast?" the birthday girl asked.

I knew there was no way I could go back to sleep. I was also fully sober for the first time in maybe a week, a week where I did not consume a single meal, the repercussions of which were all hitting me at the same time. Therefore, her idea seemed like the only thing that I wanted to do now.

I let her know about my drug-induced fast, upon hearing which she became furious. She yelled, "Everyone does benders, but that doesn't mean that you fucking don't eat or sleep for weeks. What the fuck is wrong with you? You really should eat right now. What do you have in the fridge?"

"Umm…I don't think there is anything else except beers," I said embarrassingly.

Sighing with annoyance she exclaimed, "You men are so stupid! Let me take a look into your kitchen to see if we can put something together."

I tried to give her a look conveying that I was sorry, but after seeing her reaction, I don't think she got the message.

While the birthday girl was in the kitchen gathering random ingredients to make breakfast with, I was pacing in my bedroom thinking about the sleep paralysis I had. I could not stop thinking about the floating bunny man. I started to relive the whole experience, which was interrupted by something I was not expecting. I heard a knock, though it did not come from the door. Then another knock and another, continuing every few seconds. It took me some time to figure out where they were coming from, only to realize that they were coming from my head. Someone was knocking in my head, trying to come in. I was sure it was not X as he had never knocked before or asked for permission. The same dread got over me that I felt in my sleep paralysis, making me question if the knocking was done by the bunny man.

I lit up a cigarette to try to calm down and think rationally. I remembered that I had stopped taking my medication, and it made sense that I was hearing such things. There was a pattern to my mental illness while not on meds; I would get extremely manic, and if I let that mania go on then I would start experiencing hallucinations and delusions, which got worse as time went on. Thinking of mania, I realized that I was not only sober from drugs but also not at all manic. I also noticed that my vision had a different shade of orange tint to it, it was scary orange. I had to do something before I became completely non-functional. I had two options, either to start my medication again or force more mania upon me.

I was definitely feeling the adverse effects of stopping my meds, but it also had a huge benefit to it. I was able to think freely again. My imagination was back, and I was able to navigate to different parts of my mind to think and feel. I could not let this go. To be able to think without restrictions was the only way I was ever going to find God. Therefore, I kept the idea of meds as a last resort. And there I was, facing the same problem once again. How do I get manic?

As every other time, I put on Exit music by Radiohead on my phone, hoping it should be enough. I tried to soak in every note of the song.

"Nice song!"

I heard from the kitchen. I had completely forgotten about the birthday girl. Her being in the house made it way more difficult to achieve what I wanted to. My next step was going to be cutting, which I could not do while she was in the house.

I made my way to the kitchen to talk to her trying to distract myself. I maintained composure and asked her, "So, did you find anything in the kitchen to make breakfast with?"

She smilingly answered, "Not exactly, but I found some things which might be expired, but I think we will be good. Can you pass me the salt, please?"

I picked up the salt to see that my hands were trembling. I took a deep breath and held the saltshaker in front of her.

She looked at my hands and stated, "Your hands are shaking. Are you okay? Still shaken up by the sleep paralysis?"

And as if the bunny man was listening to our conversations, he knocked right at that moment. I had to come clean to her or kick her out. Every successive knock was one step towards complete insanity. The birthday girl had been very understanding of my situation till this point, so I gave being honest a go.

I told her, "I have been hearing some things since I woke up today. It seems like it is getting worse very fast."

She paused stirring the pot for a second to say, "Okay. And how are you going to deal with this?"

I calmly answered, "I need to get manic again."

She looked me in the eyes and asked, "And how exactly are you going to do that?"

I did not want to answer the question, but in the name of honesty, I did, "Well, in this particular case, I need to hurt myself. I generally do that by cutting my arm. And I am sorry to say this. I need to do it in the next couple of minutes, and if it makes you uncomfortable, it will be better for you to leave."

She seemed offended and amused at the same time. She took a few seconds and gave a light chuckle. "Look at this," she said, lifting her skirt a bit to reveal more cut marks than I could count. Some of them looked relatively fresh. "It is totally fine with me if you do that, sometimes I do it just because I am bored. I can join you in a nice cutting session if you want," she exclaimed.

I was very pleased upon seeing and hearing this. A sense of comfort came over me. I let her know that her offer was very nice, but I had to decline it.

She hugged me. "Do your thing," she said and turned back to making breakfast from expired ingredients.

Even though the situation felt a bit odd and confusing, it was the best outcome that I could have expected. I did feel a bit weird cutting myself in front of her, so I picked up a knife that she was not using to cook and started walking to my room to do the deed. Upon almost entering the room I heard, "It is totally fine if you want to do it in front of me. I would not mind at all." I knew she was trying to make me feel comfortable, but it was not really working.

I yelled jokingly, "Let me be in peace, you bitch." I walked inside the room and shut the door behind me.

I sat on my bed and rolled up my sleeve. I looked at the cut marks from before, and even that sight gave me a slight rush of blood to my head. I put the knife right above those three marks and pressed gently on the skin. I started to taste the high I was chasing. I made a relatively deep cut going slowly from one side of my arm to another. My heart started racing faster than it did on grams of coke. The high started building slowly, but it started to gain pace in a couple of seconds. This was enough to achieve the manic state I wanted to; however, I did know that I had a small window of time to kickstart my mania. The song I chose for the job was The Trial by Pink Floyd. I also lit up a cigarette to enhance the experience and was just lost without a single thought in my mind, feeling the high rushing through me, in some sort of a meditative state. 5 minutes and 18 seconds later, when the song was over, I came back to reality as a different man. I was in the perfect manic state I wanted to be. I focused on my thoughts trying to figure out if I was still hearing the knocks, but they were not there. I felt ecstatic to find a loophole in my illness. My sight went towards the knife I was holding in my hand. Even though I did not need to cut anymore, a sense of addiction came over me, and it felt impossible to put the knife down. I made two more light cuts to get me through the day. It was one of the best cutting sessions of my life.

I went back to the kitchen and saw that the birthday girl had finished cooking.

She looked at me and said excitedly, "You look way better."

"I *feel* way better," I replied with a smirk.

She asked me if I was ready for food, to which I nodded, and she proceeded to put two forks in the frying pan, picked up the pan, and put it on the coffee table. I let her know that I had plates, upon which she went on a rant about plates from which I zoned out. Looking at the food, I had no idea what it was, but it tasted quite good, given the circumstances.

The birthday girl initiated the conversation by asking me how my cutting went. Even though I had no problems talking about such topics, she seemed way too comfortable with it; like she has such conversations on a regular basis. I was not going to give up my chance to speak freely, so I let her know in great detail about what happened in my room. She was gaining pleasure as I spoke, in some senses like a second-hand high. After listening to my experience, she got curious about my cutting history and ended up asking me about the first time I cut myself. I did not have to think a lot to answer this question, as I thought about that moment a lot, trying to relive the high I got from the first cut I had ever made on myself.

I answered with a nostalgic smile, "I was maybe 11-12 years old, and life seemed very difficult at the time. You could call me an emo kid; like My Chemical Romance and Simple Plan kind of emo. I never thought that I would cut myself; I was too scared of the concept of pain. Then there was this one day when I had a massive fight with my mom, and I was sitting in my room listening to Welcome to My Life by Simple Plan, trying to get the emotion to cry and feel worse about myself. There was a box cutter lying on the study table that I had used to make a school project. I hatched a plan to cut myself and show it to my mom to make her feel bad. But when I did cut myself, it was something beautiful. I had never been drunk or high before that, so this was the first time I had ever felt a rush of dopamine. I did not care about showing the cut to my mom anymore, I had even forgotten about the fight. All I wanted was for that feeling which I did not have a name for to never go away. And my life changed at that moment."

The birthday girl looked disappointed by that story. I asked her, "What? Is this story not up to your standards?".

She sighed and said, "You seem like a person who doesn't do things for such stupid reasons. I thought you would be the same as a child."

I preached jokingly, "Can you please not prosecute the kid me for not being ultra-stoic? I am so offended."

She laughed and claimed that her story was short but exactly how she wanted it to be.

"Let's hear it," I said.

She took a deep breath and said, "So, this is very simple. I think I was around the same age too. It happened in my school during a class when the boy sitting next to me handed me a razor and dared me to cut myself. I did not think much of it, so I did it, which made the boy freak out, and the motherfucker told the teacher about it. I was sent to the school counsellor who tried to 'counsel' me, of which I don't remember anything. I went back home and felt the need to do it again, which I did, and just never stopped until today. I don't think I get as high as you, but it does feel beautiful."

I chuckled, "You were right, that is definitely the better story to tell."

Both of us laughed and then sat in silence for a while thinking about our great cutting adventures.

She broke the silence by asking, "Have you thought about where in your pleasure scale would cutting be?"

I had not thought of that. I took some time to think and answered, "It is surely not entertainment, that is obvious. I have lived without cutting for a long time, but I cannot live without cigarettes, so I would put it below cigarettes. I think even though it gives a stronger rush of dopamine, I will still put art above it."

She nodded, "That does make sense. Also, did you notice how both of us described cutting to be beautiful? Would it not be the case that your highest pleasure or 'God' would be the most beautiful thing in the world?"

I replied with contempt, "That is a nice avenue to explore, but the only problem with it is that I do not know what beauty exactly entails to quantify it."

"What do you mean exactly?" she asked curiously.

I, not knowing whether I was going to make sense, preached, "I think beauty loses its value over time. If we look at a physical form of beauty like a great painting, it will start to lose its core essence of beauty, if it was in my living room, where I saw it almost all the time. Going on to the abstract sense of beauty, I could argue that if I cut myself all the time, it would have diminishing results, and maybe after some time it would not feel beautiful. Maybe you already feel this way. So basically, what I am trying to say is any object of beauty, physical or abstract, would lose its value if you experience it frequently, making it very difficult to put it in my search for God."

She seemed to be perplexed by my thoughts, but she humoured me saying, "I do not completely agree with it, but for the sake of the conversation, let's see where this line of thought ends up. According to you, things or feelings or whatever seem stagnant after being in your life for a while, and hence lose their beauty, right?"

I affirmed, "That is one way of saying it."

She continued, "But what about an object or feeling that changes over time?"

"If the change is repetitive, then I would face the same problem, just the beauty will diminish over a larger period of time," I replied.

"And what if the change is not repetitive?" she inquired curiously.

I stated the obvious, "Such a thing does not exist."

She sighed, "That is also true. But what if we are going at it wrong? What if the real beauty for you is just the concept of change itself?"

I questioned, "If that was the case, why do I find cutting beautiful? Or certain films? Or even cigarettes?"

"For the sake of the argument, let's try and find out. It could be argued that cutting changes your state of mind, I would agree with that from experience. Films are kind of an obvious one, it changes the world you live in. Cigarette is a bit difficult, but it could be argued that it is something you do to pause the world, changing your state of mind and your world at the same time."

"You do realize how you are sounding, right?" I yelled firmly. I continued, "This all seems very farfetched, with almost no ground to stand on."

"I know it is, but maybe something to think about in the future," she said calmly. She then abruptly ended the conversation by asking if she could shower at my place.

I told her, "Yeah sure. I would also appreciate some time to think about our conversation." She smiled and hopped off.

8

DRIVE

I could not stop thinking about the birthday girl's argument on beauty. I could not find a solid ground to put the theory on, but it did make me wonder if I needed to figure out the meaning of beauty. It did seem right that the pleasure I was looking to mix with my mania, would need to be something that I would find intrinsically beautiful. I just did not know what that word was supposed to mean.

The theory of beauty being change itself also made me think about how it would work with mania as mania was the one thing, I truly found beautiful. I felt stupid even thinking about this question because the very next second I realized that mania is the biggest change that occurs in my life. I did not want to admit it, but I was being drawn in by the idea that the birthday girl had incepted in my mind.

In midst of my inner monologue, I hear the birthday girl shout, "Hey, is it cool if I wear your clothes?"

I told her that it was fine and that she could take anything from the closet. She came back to the couch a minute later wearing my T-shirt which had 'Let's get weird' written on it. She complimented me on the T-shirt, and with one look at my face, she knew I was in deep thought.

She asked, "Are you still thinking about that conversation?" I nodded. "Let this go for today. You have a lot of time to find your God. Let's do something fun today, it is my birthday still after all." She said firmly.

I had completely forgotten about her birthday. I apologised to her profusely and went on to ask if I could buy her some coke as a gift. She accepted the apology and the offering of coke.

I texted dealer 1 asking for three grams of coke; he replied within a minute, letting me know that he was close by and will come over in about 5 minutes. I picked up a half-empty bottle of fancy vodka I had by the couch and poured two shots into the dirty glasses I had on the coffee table. I picked one glass up, gave the other to the birthday girl and said, "Happy birthday to the only person I have met who is cool enough to weird me out. Let's get weird."

She smiled as we clinked our glasses and took the first shot of the day.

I asked the birthday girl if she wanted to do something particular on her birthday. She answered with a grin on her face, "I would love to get fucked up and go on a drive."

Even though I did not particularly like leaving my apartment, drunk driving was right up my alley. It was something that I would do regularly, even without a destination to go to. I told her I was very excited about that idea, and right then the doorbell rang. I knew it was dealer 1, so I took the cash out of my wallet and opened the door. Dealer 1 never made small talk, so right there at the entrance of my apartment, I gave him the cash, and procured the three grams of cocaine.

I got back to the couch to see that the birthday girl was already making our next shots. She passed me my shot and asked for the coke. She took her shot and rubbed a bit of coke on her gums as a chaser. She swore by coke was the best chaser out there and asked me to give it a try. Upon trying it, it was obvious to me that I was an old-fashioned man who liked the coca cola kind of coke as his chaser.

I emptied the bag of coke onto the mirror on the coffee table to crush it, but it already was very finely crushed. Generally, the quality of coke would be worse if I got it crushed from the dealer as it would be easier to mix other substances in it, but sometimes it surprised me, and I was really hoping for this to be one of those times.

I asked the birthday girl how big she wanted the lines, to which she shrugged, "I don't really care, whatever you want really."

"Big it is then," I stated. I cut 8 big lines on the mirror, going from one end to another. I picked up the straw holding it in from of her saying, "Birthday girl goes first."

She chuckled, "You said this to me last night, and it is probably the reason why I am here right now."

Both of us let out a laugh. She picked up the straw, and slowly snorted her line while I held her hair back. When she got up, she looked a bit perplexed and asked, "Why did you make eight lines already?"

I answered with a smirk, "After these eight lines, we are going to go on a drive, and the rest we do while driving."

She was very pleased by that answer, so pleased that she made two more shots. I did my line before drinking my shot, and a line just after, to see if snorting coke was a better chaser. It was not. She got curious about this chaser, so she made two more shots, which both of us drank at the same time, but she chased it with coke while I used coca cola. I asked her if she wanted a cigarette, and upon hearing which a sense of relief came over her.

She yelled, "Yes, please."

I took out my pack, and gave her one saying, "Here is your cancer stick." I flicked one in my mouth. I lit hers first, and then mine. It was a nice break from the drug consumption. Both of us sat in complete silence for the whole duration of the cigarette; like we were best friends, even though we had just met 12 hours ago.

As I was putting out my cigarette in the overflowing ashtray, she asked me, "Shot or line?"

"Why not both?" was the obvious answer.

Two more shots were made, but this time we did our lines before the shots, which my body did not like.

There we were, two of us, with two lines on the mirror, and enough vodka in the bottle for two more shots. There was nothing to wait for, she, like a force of habit poured the last shots, which we drank and did our lines, ending the mandatory addict birthday rituals.

I turned to her excitedly, "So are we ready for a drive?"

"Yes, I am, but do you have a car? That might be necessary." She questioned.

"I don't, but I can rent one from this app I have," I answered.

She seemed thrilled, and yelled, "Let's go!"

I packed up the rest of the coke on the mirror in the bag that the dealer had given us, booked a car from the car renting app, made another two shots for good measures, which we drank in an instant and stood up to be on our way. Upon standing up I felt a bit dizzy and murmured, "I am a bit more fucked up than I thought I was."

"Yeah, so am I," she replied with a laugh.

The car pick-up point was right outside my front door, which was fortunate because neither of us was in a state to walk a long distance. As we approached the pick-up point, we saw that the car I had booked in a drunken state was a hot pink, convertible Mini Cooper.

The birthday girl glared at me stating, "You make good drunk decisions."

We entered the car, put the seatbelts on, she played The Cult of Dionysus by The Orion Experience as the first song of the road trip and we were on our way to nowhere.

I knew a highway that generally did not have much traffic at any point of the day, so I turned the car over there. The birthday girl was without a care about where we were going, she was enjoying herself, dancing and singing every word of the song. I soon joined her with the singing and even started to steer with my legs, so that I could dance with my hands. In between her dance, she stopped, turned to me and shouted, "We need to do coke."

I took out the bag from my pocket which I handed to her with my wallet saying, "Just use any card to do bumps."

She scraped some coke from the corner of the card and did a bump, then she scraped some more coke from the card, and put it next to my nose so I could snort while driving. She got visibly more energetic by that small bump, and so did I. Luckily it was one of those times when pre crushed coke was good, I thought. She put on a heavy metal song that I had not heard before while riling with energy. She insisted that I drove faster, and I happily obliged. I floored the accelerator and tried to see what speed I was at, but I was so drunk that the speedometer did not make much sense. As I was approaching a turn, I looked from the corner of my eye that the birthday girl was making another bump, but as the car turned, the coke fell from the card, making her very mad, demanding that we find a better way to do this. I told her that I did not know of a better way to do coke while driving when an idea sparked in her head. She started going through her bag and found an empty box of tic tac. I was curious to see what was happening, so I slowed the car down to look at what she was doing. She took the lid out of the box, filled it three quarters with coke, put the lid back on, rolled up a banknote, and put the note in the hole of the lid from where the tic tacs were supposed to come out. She continued to easily snort from it and passed the greatest feat of drug engineering to me. I gave it a snort, getting the perfect amount of coke that I wanted. I wanted to compliment her, but I had no words for this saint who was sitting next to me. So, I just went back to driving fast.

We spoke almost no words as we were busy singing and dancing our hearts out while taking tic tac bumps every five minutes, but our session stopped when the birthday girl went into a deep thought. I turned down the volume in the car to ask what she had in her mind; she answered my question with another question. "Have you ever tried to commit suicide?"

This was a topic that I tried to avoid in most conversations, not because it was taboo or in some senses dark, but because the thought of death was the only personal thing I had in my life. But on the other hand, if there was anyone, I would want to share such intimate thoughts with, it would be the birthday girl, so in the spirit of our short friendship, I answered truthfully, "I have attempted suicide before, a couple of times, actually. What about you?"

She was hesitant to answer the question, but it seemed fairly reasonable to assume that she wanted me to ask it. After a brief pause, she confessed, "I have not made any attempts, however, I had planned to make my first attempt today. Maybe that is why I am with you still, to prolong it. Maybe if the clock hits 12 tonight, and my birthday is over, I might stop feeling this way."

I turned my focus from driving to her. I looked into her eyes and knew instantly that she was serious about it. I did not want her to die for selfish reasons, I had only known her for a day, but it was not for me to decide. I gathered up the courage to ask her if there was a reason behind this thought.

She answered very characteristically to herself, "No, I don't have a reason. Reasons and circumstances are something that comes and goes, so I don't think they should be the reason behind the biggest thought of my life. I am honestly just bored, and life just seems so overrated."

I could have comforted her by saying something a doctor would say, or I could have given her pointers from my own experience in such a situation, I could have even just assured her that I would stay with her till midnight. But I rather chose to say, "I am not letting you die without me. Let's just fucking die together."

She laughed off my enthusiastic support for death saying, "You don't mean that. Also, it is not something that you need to do."

I replied, "No, seriously. You have heard about this stupid quest I have based my entire life on, which I am never going to succeed at. I can happily die right now. I could just drive off a cliff, and we would happily be dead in the next 10 minutes."

"Okay, if you are serious take a few bumps to gather up the courage," she said while handing me the box of tic tac. I took five bumps and handed it back to her. "Are you actually serious?" she asked with every intent to go on with it if I answered yes.

I gave my answer by taking off my seatbelt. She took a deep breath, took her seatbelt off, and took a few bumps herself.

I asked with a hint of nervousness, "What is our death song?"

She was already on her phone searching for a song, and in the next 10 seconds, Dawn Chorus by Thom Yorke was played. She passed me the tic tac box for one last bump while she pressed the button to get the convertible top off. I took 3 bumps to overcome my body's need for survival and saw that the straight highway turned left in the distance.

I stated, "I am going to keep on driving straight at a high speed. We will break through the barrier and fall down the cliff. Are you still 100% sure?" I asked with a corner of my heart hoping for a different answer than the one I knew I was going to get.

She shouted, "LET'S FUCKING DO THIS!"

I put the pedal to the floor, somewhat hoping for a last-minute miracle, which came in the form of a sign from the God I was looking for. X made contact with me once again, telling me, "You cannot die right now. You have not found God yet."

I argued, saying out loud, "But you are the one who claimed that death is my God."

X replied in a soothing voice, "It is, and you need to find that out in time. God cannot be accessed so easily."

Before I could get the time to think about that sentence, the song changed to Happiness by Kasabian, throwing me off guard, and instantly getting my adrenaline down. My body, without any command from my brain, pumped the brake as hard as it could making the car slow enough to stop just before the highway barrier. Both of us felt the jerk of the small accident, but we were able to hold on to our seats.

We sat there in silence, after our almost suicide attempt, listening to Happiness. The birthday girl, breathing very heavily, took a few bumps from the box and passed it to me; I could not count the number of bumps I did. I got my box of cigarettes out, gave one to her, and lit one myself. We stayed there in the middle of the highway, smoking a cigarette, not knowing what to say to each other. She threw her cigarette out without even finishing it, put the convertible top back on and also put her seat belt back on. She comforted me saying, "This is definitely for the best, we were being stupid."

I chuckled, "Let's see what tomorrow is like."

She smiled and claimed, "I have had enough excitement for a day. Can you please drop me home?" I agreed and drove off to the address she gave me.

On the way to her house, we did not talk to each other, or listen to music. We just kept on doing bumps and passing the box to each other. After a while, we reached her tall apartment building. She asked if she could take the coke, to which I answered, "It was your gift."

She thanked me for a memorable birthday and disappeared into her building. I drove for a while to get back to my house in complete silence, but just a minute from my house, I parked the car in an empty street, put on a song I did not care to hear, and turned the volume to the maximum and I screamed. A tear even rolled down my cheek. I calmed myself down with a cigarette, and slowly made my way home.

9

HUMANITY

My house looked like it always did; there was trash all around, half drank bottles of alcohol on the floor and dirty glasses on the coffee table. Still, something seemed off in it. I looked at the shot glasses, from which the birthday girl and I were drinking, scared that she might not want to see me again. I rarely ever missed people if I did not need them, but could it be true that I was missing her in my house? 24 hours was too little time to get addicted to someone but could it be true that it was enough to make me love her?

I poured two shots of rum into the glasses we were drinking from; I took mine and clinked it with hers, hoping she would be doing the same. I make another shot in my glass, leaving hers full for her if she ever comes back into this house. I keep on repeating the process till the bottle was finally empty, leaving hers untouched still.

My body started getting warm, and my vision was dizzy. My stomach started to reject all of the poison it was forced to consume. I tried to calm it with a cigarette. The first drag seemed to do the trick, but the second one opened the door for my body to get rid of all the toxins forced upon it without its consent. I threw up violently on the couch. Before I could take a breath, my body punished me by making me gag for a few minutes without any breaks to breathe. After it was done, I was physically sober, but fortunately, my mania was still running strong.

I did not care to clean the couch or my face, which had chunks of the breakfast I ate, stuck to my beard. The only thing I cleaned was the outside of the birthday girls' glass, which had a few drops of bile mixed with vodka which I had drunk hours before. I continued smoking the cigarette which was already between my fingers to take revenge on my body. This time it did not have anything to splurge out of me, therefore it accepted its fate. I took advantage of that fact by finding a bottle of whisky and taking a shot. It also was a good time to do more coke because my heart had stopped pounding against my chest. I messaged dealer 1 for a gram of coke, but never got a reply. I called dealer 2 but his phone was turned off. As a last resort, I thought of asking my neighbour if she had any with her.

I walked to her door, my beard still covered with puke, and knocked. She had no reaction upon seeing me like that; she just greeted me, "What's up?"

I assumed she was on heroin, which was her drug of choice. I asked if she had any coke with her, to which she told me that she can go check her drug stash. I pleasantly asked her to, and she walked off bumping into the walls every few steps. I waited at the door for a couple of minutes when she came back with what looked like two grams of coke. She told me I could have it for free, and can return the favour the next time she is in need. I thanked her and went back inside my apartment.

I sat on the couch next to the pool of vomit to start doing my coke, but my body had another card it could play. It made me tired. I was so tired instantly that I could not get myself to crush the coke. I had not slept for weeks, and the first time I felt tired was after the only night I had slept. My body had made it obvious that it had started to hate me completely.

I lied on the couch over the puke which had gotten quite cold by the time. The cold or the wetness of the vomit did not bother me, but the surrounding silence did. I took out my phone to play a song while I fall asleep, but it was not charged, and I fell into darkness arguing if I should get the charger from the bedroom or not.

I woke up because of a dream I could not remember, sober enough to realise that I was sleeping on my own vomit. I did not want to deal with it, so I did not bother to clean up. I lit up a cigarette recollecting the day that

I had had. I looked up at the clock on the wall, which showed it was about 2. It was dark outside, letting me know that it was 2 am. The birthday girl's birthday was over, now she was just a girl. The conversation of ours came into my mind when she had told me that she might stop contemplating suicide after midnight. I decided to reach out to her to check up on her, and also as an excuse to stay in her life.

I walked into the bedroom, plugged my phone into the charger, and turned it on. I did not have her number, so I planned on asking B for it. When my phone was turned on it gave me notifications of two messages that I had received while it was dead. The first one was at 1:48 am from B, making me mad that I would have to reply to it to ask for the girl's number. The second one was received at 11:31 pm by an unknown number. I decided to read that first; it said, "Hey, I am sorry about today. If you don't have anything important, would you mind if I came over to yours?"

I was elated upon reading this. The girl wanted to stay in my life. And not only did she message me, but she had to find my number through B, which made me happier because she took that extra step. I replied, smiling, "I am sorry, my phone was not charged. You don't have anything to apologise for. I would love it if you come over, and we can talk about it."

I did not need B for the number anymore, therefore there was no need to read and reply to his message. But because I was so happy with the girl's message, I felt I owed him this much for introducing us. The text said, "Hey, man. You went home with the girl last night, right? She also asked for your number. It seems like you guys became quite good friends in a day. So..umm...I don't know how to say it, but maybe you should know this, she killed herself a couple of hours ago. Sorry, bro."

10

DEPRAVITY

$\mathcal{U}$pon hearing the news, I had a somewhat paradoxical reaction to it. My slowly fading mania started to rise again. A sense of heavenly euphoria came over me and I even attained some sort of sexual gratification from it. If anyone had seen me at that moment, they would have thought that I was glad upon hearing of the demise of the girl, but it was not true at all. This situation was nothing but a non-physical form of hurt inflicted upon me. I did feel bad because I could not feel bad, giving me an option to either act the way they do in films when facing the same situation, or I could use the superpowers of my mental illness to do the one thing I was put on Earth for; find God.

The decision would have been an easy one a few weeks ago. I would have cried in front of people, tell everyone how much she meant to me and maybe I would have even lied to myself to make the misery true. But I had no space in my life anymore; for people or for lies. It would be completely futile to make myself suffer while being presented with the opportunity to feel pure bliss by this unknown God. The only logical solution to the dilemma was to cut off the girl from my thoughts, which I symbolically did by drinking the shot I had poured for her because she was never going to.

The high that I had gotten from her death was exponentially more than I could get from the act of cutting. This got me thinking that what if death was indeed a very high form of pleasure like X suggested? But the problem with my death was that I would not be able to feel the pleasure of death if I were dead. The answer was right in front of me. Death need not be mine; someone else's could also do the trick.

I lit up a cigarette to take a step back and question the morality of what I was thinking. "Am I trying to convince myself that the death of others would give me pleasure?" I asked myself. My medication had been stopped for a while now, and it could have been possible that I was being delusional. But my body had just shown me the shimmer of the light I was searching for. But then again, I had another question to deal with; how I was going to find death around me to derive that pleasure? Only one answer came to me, and it was the one I feared the most. I had to kill people.

The thought of it was too much to handle, but on the other hand, it was also shooting pulses of high in my body. I made 6 lines of the coke I had taken from my neighbour and did all of them savouring every little burn I could feel in my septum. The result of this pushed me even more to do something which was morally wrong, even by my standards. I was trying to hold my mind with all my might from crossing the line it had painted with blood. But I was not strong enough.

I let go. And my mind started spiralling to a place where the likes of Ted Bundy and Jeffery Dahmer are. At that moment I called myself a serial killer. The dramatic effect of the phrase gave me another pulse of high, making my mind even dig out the rock bottom.

I walked around the apartment trying to control the high I was experiencing from such diabolical thoughts. I happened to walk in front of my mirror and looked at myself. My eyes were bloodshot, my hair wet with sweat and my beard full of puke. I looked exactly like the person my mind had convinced me to be. I closed my eyes and prayed to my God to not let this happen. And my God answered my prayers by giving me one minute of sober clarity. In that window, I came to the conclusion that I need someone's help to stop me.

I went over my phone to look for any person who could do the job, but as I had known, no one I knew in the city would help me without calling the cops. I made two more lines to keep a grip. While cutting the coke, it reminded me of the neighbour who would probably help me out. I snorted the lines, washed my face and got ready for the most awkward conversation of my life.

I went up to her door and knocked. There was no answer, so I knocked once again. I could hear footsteps approaching the door, each footstep increasing my anxiety. She finally opened the door looking confused. I asked her if she was free. She nodded, still in confusion. "I need to talk about something weird. Would you want to come over and talk over a few lines?" I asked.

"Sure," she replied, and we headed to my apartment.

I offered her a seat on the couch next to the dried vomit; she did not hesitate in taking the seat. I cut four lines and pulled up my balls to start talking. "So, first of all, please don't freak out about whatever I am going to say," I said after snorting a line.

"All right," she said with politeness while taking the straw from me.

I waited for her to do her line and then claimed, "I am just saying it outright. I feel like killing people."

She stared at me with a slight hint of fear. "Are you going to kill me?" she chuckled.

I let out a light laugh and told her, "Quite the opposite, actually. I do not want to do it, but my mind is forcing me to, so I need you to put some sense in me."

She looked straight at the tv for a solid minute and broke her silence to say, "I could do that. Or you could kill the known predators in the area. Like some Dexter type person."

I looked at her in disbelief and rhetorically asked, "Are you fucking serious?"

I assumed that at this point she would laugh and tell me that she was kidding, but she said, very seriously, "I have an ice pick you could use."

"See, I am very very very interested in this idea, but I will try to talk myself out of it tonight, and if that doesn't work out, I will come to you tomorrow."

She had no problem with that, so she did a line, said goodnight and went back.

I was in the same place where I had started once again, maybe even worse than that. I could not find any logic which could end this craving. I decided to do the simplest thing to get my mind off it, watch a film. Going through my list of films I found *Donnie Darko*. It used to be my favourite childhood film. I thought maybe watching that would make me relive my childhood and relinquish the evil brewing in my head.

I pressed play, and watched the whole film in complete amazement, completely sure that destiny had made me watch it. The film contained the answer to all of my problems. My God had shown it to me.

The bunny man in the film was the same one who had haunted me in my sleep and knocked on my brain which I had never answered because I had thought it was there to hurt me. But I was wrong. Completely wrong. He was my guide sent from my God to show me the way, just like it had done in the film. The answer of God was so obvious in that instance. I felt like I knew the answer all along, but I ignored all the signs because I was scared. But now I could see the concept of fear flying away from my body. Then I finally said it, "God is death. My death."

11

SCARLET LINES

I composed myself from the celestial elation flowing through me like the river in the Garden of Eden. I knew what I had to do, but the question remained on how to do it. I did not want it to be instant, and I did not want to be asleep because I wanted to live through the divine experience. I had the option of hanging myself or cutting my arm up.

In reverence to my pleasure of cutting, I chose that to be the option. I went to the bathroom and ran hot water into the bathtub. While the tub was getting full, I started doing coke. Line after line after line. I did not stop until I could hear water overflowing from the tub. I did my last line and paid respect to my favourite drug.

I took the sharpest knife that I had and placed it next to the tub. I put my cigarettes and my white lighter next to the knife. I played Comfortably Numb on repeat and put the phone carefully on the sink. I stripped all my clothes and entered the tub. I lit up a cigarette, fantasizing about what was to come, and remembering my whole journey. I was going to get the highest pleasure in the world. I thanked X, apologized for not listening to him earlier, and surprisingly got a reply, "The journey was yours to take."

My vision got progressively orange with each drag of my cigarette, and by the end of it, the bunny man had appeared next to the tub. Not to frighten me, but rather to comfort me in my truest moment. "It is time," he spoke.

I nodded and picked up my knife to see that he was gone. So was X. It was clear that I had to walk the rest of the path by myself.

I put the tip of the knife above my wrist and cut to my elbow. I bled a bit, but it was still a superficial cut. I put the tip on the same spot once again and pressed as hard as I could, in the same motion I did previously. I flinched for one second with pain, but when I opened my eyes, I saw blood flow through the tub, colouring the water in an angelic red colour. At that moment, I could not help but remember the conversation I had with the girl about beauty. I was looking at it, lying in a tub filled with bloody water with a wound that could only be described as God's stamp. It was my definition of beauty.

My vision was as red as the blood being pumped from my arm. The feeling I felt was something that words could not do justice to. It was the highest form of pleasure achievable.

The Scarlet Lines on my arm paved the path on which I walked towards the darkness, surrounded by light.